The Sharing Frog

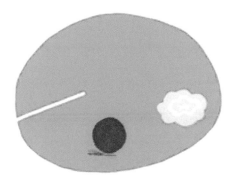

By Julia Pelon

The

Sharing

Frog

First Printing, 2021

ISBN

979-8-65088-001-1

Dedication:

To my three cowboys:
Joshua, Caleb, and Josiah,
the best sons in the world.

**Ernie is a green frog
who lives on a great big lake.**

**Every day, Ernie sits
on his favorite lily pad,**

eating his favorite food,

swimming,

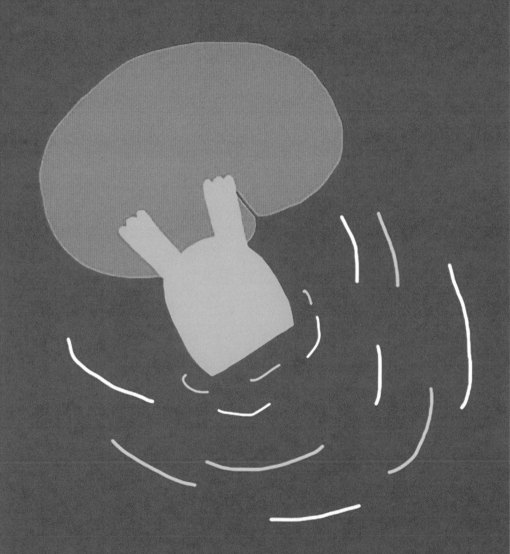

and playing with his friends.

Day after day, Ernie had so much fun.

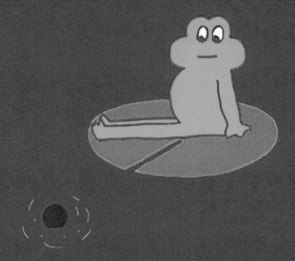

One day, when Ernie was sitting on his
lily pad, he looked down and saw something
unusual. It was a big, red berry floating
in the water.

"Ooh, so shiny, and it bounces too!"
Ernie thought.

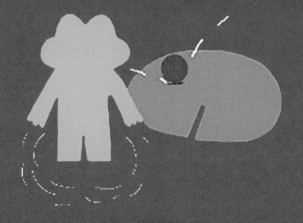

Ernie played with his new toy
all morning.

But when his friends came to play,
Ernie hid it in the tall grass.

"I can't share my new toy with them..
It's mine, and, they might take it,
or lose it," Ernie thought.

So when Ernie's friends came, they asked
excitedly, "Can we play with you?"
"Uh, no," Ernie said quietly.
"I don't want to."
Sadly, Ernie's friends swam away,
and Ernie was left alone.

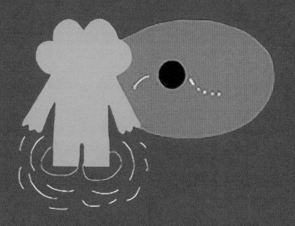

Ernie started playing with his berry again. It suddenly didn't seem so shiny, or bouncy as it was before.

Ernie remembered God doesn't want him to be selfish. God is loving and sharing and He wants him to be like that too.

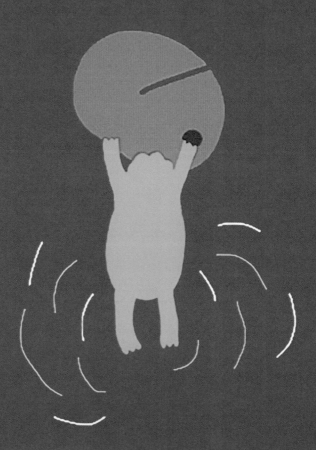

**Ernie grabbed his special toy
and quickly swam away
to find his friends.**

"Hey guys, look what I have!
Would you like to play with me?"
Ernie eagerly asked.

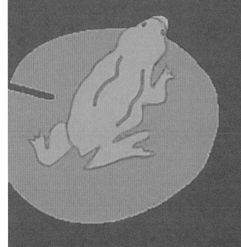

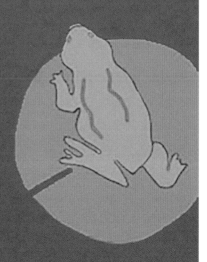

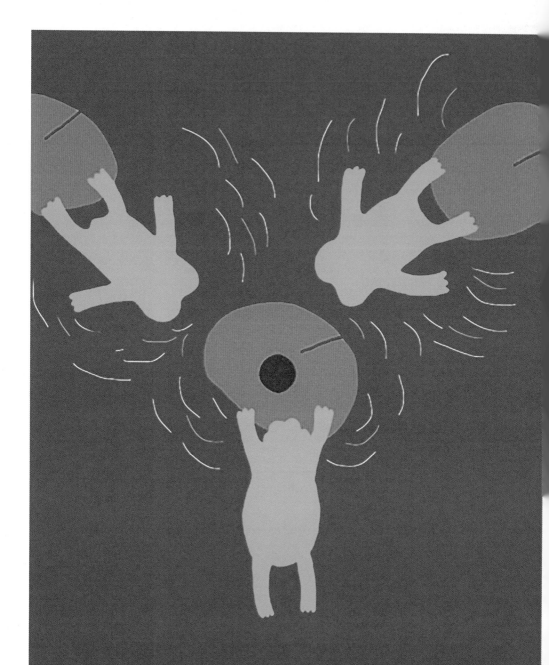

"Sure!" yelled his friends.
Ernie and his friends had so much fun
as they shared and played together
all afternoon.

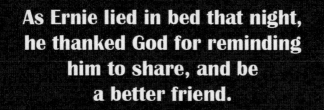

As Ernie lied in bed that night,
he thanked God for reminding
him to share, and be
a better friend.

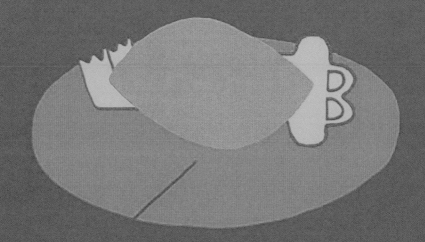

THE

END

But do not forget to do good and
to share, for with such sacrifices
God is well pleased.

Hebrews 13:16

Fun Ideas and Activities to Compliment

The Sharing Frog

I'm a teacher also, so I LOVE children, I LOVE books, I LOVE activities, and I LOVE fun! I decided to add some things that you can read or do with children that would make this amazing book even more fun. Enjoy!

List of Contents

Science and Math

1. Berry study: what kinds of berries are red?
   - list, study, draw, taste

2. Qualities and nutritional benefits of berries

3. Discuss dry measures: pint, quart, peck, bushel

4. Do berries bounce? Test, measure, chart

5. Money Study: counting, sorting, naming; playing store for a Produce Stand

6. Cooking: make recipes with berries

   * Cranberry Bars

   * Strawberry Shortcake

   * Berry Smoothie

   * Jam on crackers or

     homemade bread

   * Butter Jam Cookies

7. Taste and Guess Game with a variety of berries

8. Frog Study: types, sizes, development, locations, habitats

9. Food Chain

10. Study frog behavior: independent and in a group

11. Adopt a frog: research and care for a frog

Art

1. Berry Painting
2. Berry Dyeing
3. Marble painting
4. Berry and leaf wreath collage
5. Make a frog sharing page with moveable ball
6. Hand prints on paper with paint- "I share with these hands"
7. Make a card for Grandparents or other relatives, expressing love and thoughtfulness
8. Strawberry Basket crafts: weave with yarn or ribbon

9. Make a giving container out of a can that can be decorated
10. Make a gospel tract to share God with others
11. Make a Frog Life Cycle paper wheel
12. Make a necklace for mom out of macaroni or beads
13. Make "Kindness Bags" for the hungry

Music and Movement

1. Sing "Jesus Loves the Little Children"
2. Sing "He's Got the Whole World in His Hands"
3. Play games with different kinds of balls
4. Play "Share the Potato"
5. Play Hide and Seek with a ball
6. Bounce a ball to each other in a circle, and every time it's your turn, say, "Jesus loves me", or "God likes it when I share"
7. Play with bubbles- do they bounce?

Character Building

1. Discuss sharing vs. selfishness
2. Discuss giving vs. taking
3. Discuss friendship
4. Discuss love
5. Discuss God's love
6. Discuss thankfulness
7. Discuss sharing- it's not always easy, but what pleases God
    - share blessings
    - thinking of others
    - God calls us to share with people in need
    - God calls us to share our love with family and others

Stories from the Bible

1. Boy sharing his lunch: Matthew 14: 14-21
2. Shunamite woman: 2 Kings 4: 8-11
3. Believers sharing with those in need: Acts 4: 33-35
4. Creating the Tabernacle: Exodus 35: 21-36: 1-6
5. Ananias and Sapphira: Acts 4: 34- 5: 11

Sharing Scriptures

Psalm 112: 5

A good man deals graciously and lends; He
will guide his affairs with discretion.

Proverbs 3: 9-10

Honor the Lord with your possessions, and
with the first fruits of all your increase; so
your barns will be filled with plenty, and
your vats will overflow with new wine.

Proverbs 11: 25

The generous soul will be made rich, and he
who waters will also be watered himself.

Proverbs 11: 24

There is one who scatters, yet increases
more; and there is one who withholds more
than in right, but it leads to poverty.

Proverbs 19: 17

He who has pity on the poor lends to the
Lord, and He will pay back what he has
given.

Proverbs 22: 9

He who has a generous eye will be blessed,
for he gives of his bread to the poor.

Proverbs 31: 20

She extends her hands to the poor, yes, she
reaches out her hands to the needy.

Isaiah 32: 8

But a generous man devises generous
things, and by generosity he shall stand.

Luke 6: 38

Give, and it will be given to you: good
measure, pressed down, shaken together,
and running over will be put into your
bosom. For with the same measure that you
use, it will be measured back to you.

Proverbs 21: 26

He covets greedily all day long, but the
righteous gives and does not spare.

*New King James Version

Sharing Testimonies

This is the place where you write down the times you had to share. You did, and it really made someone happy!

1.

2.

3.

4.

5.

6.

7.

8.

9.

Made in the USA
Columbia, SC
10 June 2022

61520705R00022